• FOLK TALES FROM AROUND THE WORLD •

The Unhappy Stonecutter

A Japanese Folk Tale

written by Charlotte Guillain ✺ illustrated by Steve Dorado

Raintree is an imprint of Capstone Global Library Limited, a company incorporated in England and Wales having its registered office at 7 Pilgrim Street, London, EC4V 6LB – Registered company number: 6695582

www.raintree.co.uk
myorders@raintree.co.uk

Edited by Daniel Nunn, Rebecca Rissman, Sian Smith, and Gina Kammer
Designed by Joanna Hinton-Malivoire and Peggie Carley
Original illustrations © Capstone Global Library Ltd 2014
Illustrated by Steve Dorado
Production by Victoria Fitzgerald
Originated by Capstone Global Library Ltd
Printed and bound in China by RR Donnelley Asia

ISBN 978 1 406 28130 9 (paperback)
18 17 16 15 14
10 9 8 7 6 5 4 3 2 1

ISBN 978 1 406 28137 8 (big book)
18 17 16 15 14
10 9 8 7 6 5 4 3 2 1

British Library Cataloguing in Publication Data
A full catalogue record for this book is available from the British Library.

Characters

Haru, the stonecutter

Mountain spirit

A long time ago, a stonecutter called Haru lived in Japan.

Every day, Haru climbed up the mountain to cut away stone and carve it into statues for his customers.

Haru was a happy man. He heard stories of a spirit that came down from the mountain and granted wishes. Haru took no notice of the stories because he did not wish for anything.

But one day, Haru took a statue he had carved to a rich man's house. As he entered the house, he looked around at all the beautiful things the rich man owned. Haru wished that he were rich too.

As soon as Haru had made his wish, the spirit from the mountain granted it! When he got home, his house was much bigger, and it was full of expensive things. Haru felt very happy, and he did not have to work anymore.

One day, the sun was so hot that Haru had to stay indoors. As he looked out of the window, he saw a prince pass by in a carriage with servants holding umbrellas over his head.

Haru wished he were
a prince too.

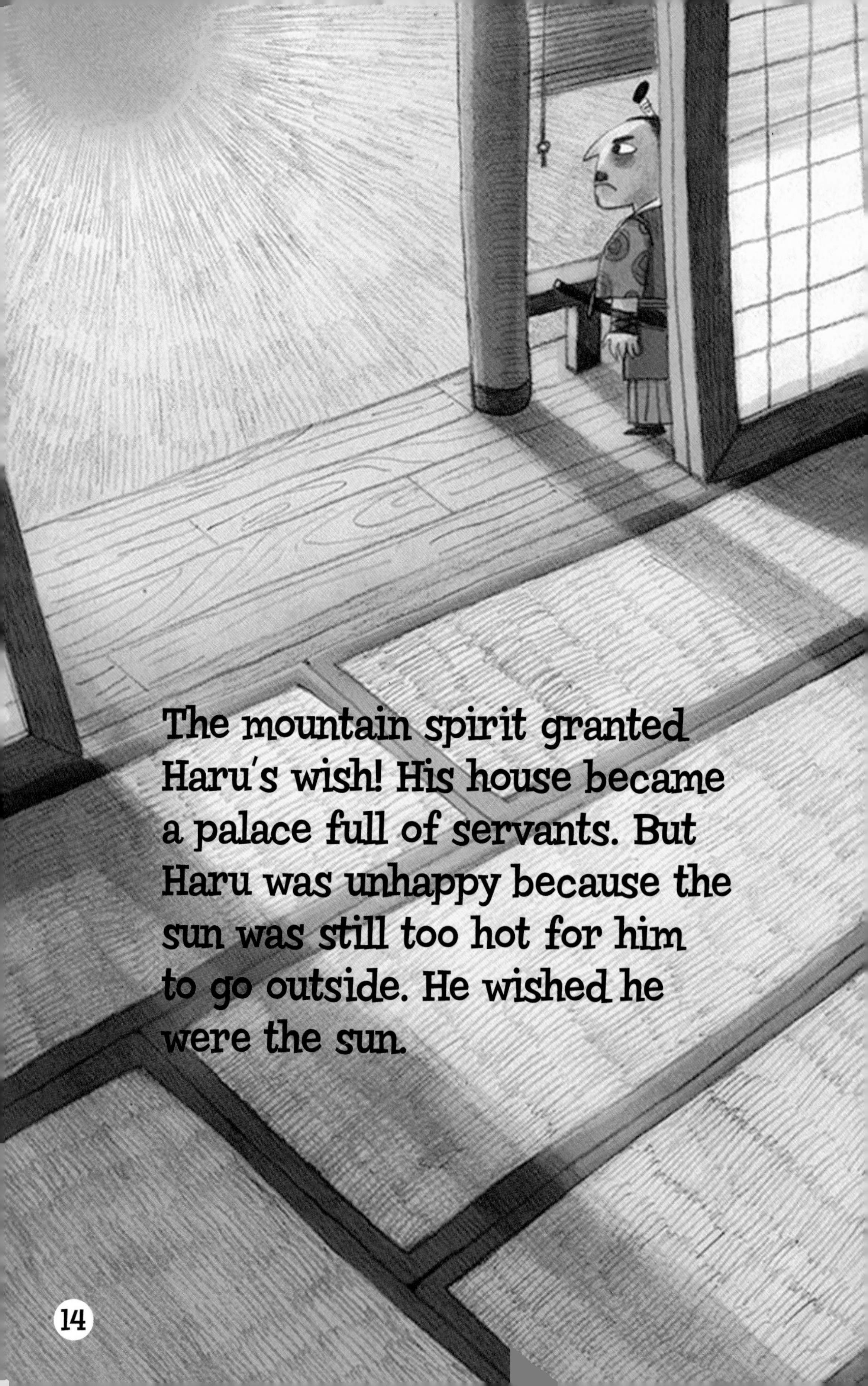

The mountain spirit granted Haru's wish! His house became a palace full of servants. But Haru was unhappy because the sun was still too hot for him to go outside. He wished he were the sun.

Again the mountain spirit granted Haru's wish! He became the sun and made the grass and the crops in the fields wither and die.

But then a cloud passed by and blocked his rays. Haru was furious! He wished he were a cloud.

Once more his wish was granted, and Haru became a cloud.

He rained down on Earth, flooding the land and washing away almost everything.

But he could not wash away the mountain. So then Haru wished he were the mountain.

Haru's wish was granted again, and he became the mountain. But one day a stonecutter climbed up the mountain and started chipping away at the rock.

Haru wished he were
a stonecutter.

The spirit granted his wish, and Haru was a stonecutter once more. He worked hard, and his life was simple.

But Haru was happy, and he never wished for anything ever again.

The end

The moral of the story

Many traditional stories have a moral. This is a lesson you can learn from the story. The moral of this story is that you should count your blessings and be grateful for who you are and what you already have. This story also warns us to be careful what we wish for!

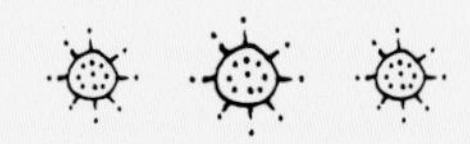

The origins of *The Unhappy Stonecutter*

Nobody knows who first told the story of *The Unhappy Stonecutter*, but the story comes from Japan. People used to tell stories like this for entertainment before we had television, radio, or computers. The story has been passed on by Japanese storytellers over hundreds of years, with different storytellers making their own changes to it over time. Eventually, people began to write the story down, and so it has spread around the world.